The Litter Critter

Sharon Lee

authorHOUSE®

AuthorHouse™ UK Ltd.
500 Avebury Boulevard
Central Milton Keynes, MK9 2BE
www.authorhouse.co.uk
Phone: 08001974150

©2011 Sharon Lee. All rights reserved.

No part of this book may be reproduced, stored in a retrieval system, or transmitted by any means without the written permission of the author.

First published by AuthorHouse   4/4/2011

ISBN: 978-1-4567-7699-2 (sc)

Any people depicted in stock imagery provided by Thinkstock are models, and such images are being used for illustrative purposes only. Certain stock imagery © Thinkstock.

This book is printed on acid-free paper.

Because of the dynamic nature of the Internet, any web addresses or links contained in this book may have changed since publication and may no longer be valid. The views expressed in this work are solely those of the author and do not necessarily reflect the views of the publisher, and the publisher hereby disclaims any responsibility for them.

Contents

Chapter 1: Pinderton	1
Chapter 2: Litter is Litter	3
Chapter 3: A Fishy Tale	5
Chapter 4: Poor Amber (part 1)	7
Chapter 5: Bright Eyes	8
Chapter 6: Poor Amber (part 2)	10
Chapter 7: At School	12
Chapter 8: Fish & Chips	14
Chapter 9: Rumbles in the Night	16
Chapter 10: Vanishing Litter	18
Chapter 11: The Park Visitor	20
Chapter 12: What Rubbish!	22
Chapter 13: The Litter Critter	24
Chapter 14: The Birth of a Litter Critter	27
Chapter 15: The School Visitor	29
Chapter 16: The Headteacher's Office	31
Chapter 17: Emergency Assembly	33
Chapter 18: Daylight Outing	35
Chapter 19: Town Hall Meeting	38
Chapter 20: The Solution	40

Chapter 1: Pinderton

What's your town like, where you live? Is it clean and tidy or is it a bit messy, with lots of rubbish lying around? Well, this story is about a beautiful town called Pinderton, right in the middle of England, where all the streets and playing fields are clean and tidy – and about it's mysterious secret that a young boy called Mark discovered by accident one evening…

Pinderton is very probably much like your town – it has a school, a park, a playing field (where most boys play football), a church and some shops. Not really very unusual so far, is it? Oh – and Pinderton doesn't seem to have any trouble with litter. It's not that nobody ever drops any litter, they do, but the litter doesn't seem to stay there for very long. It just seems to be a town that always looks spotlessly tidy – as if a magical cleaning lady comes in the night and tidies everything up ready for the next day!

Mark and his friends were in Year 3 at Pinderton Primary School; his teacher, Mr Stanton, was a rather odd teacher and Mark couldn't make up his mind whether he liked him or not. He was always in one of two moods - either cross, sitting at his desk and shouting at the class or he was happy and excited, jumping around the classroom – a very odd teacher indeed. One day Mark was at school and this morning Mr Stanton was teaching them about science – Mark wasn't really very interested in science, his favourite lesson was PE, but today, he was paying attention because his teacher had just said something that Mark thought he must have misheard; either that or Mr Stanton had gone quite mad! And if you thought your teacher had gone mad, well, you would want to listen wouldn't you – is there anything funnier than a teacher that's talking nonsense? Well, Mark heard his teacher say that he was going to show them how to create living creatures! Really – that's what he said! They were going to carry out an experiment to create life – right there in the classroom! Apparently, so Mr Stanton carried on, it can't happen in one lesson, so they would start today and in a month they would look at their experiments and see if anyone had managed to create a living creature. Gosh, Mark was excited – they'd never done anything like this before at school. He wondered what he wanted to create…maybe a dog, he'd always wanted a dog? No, he thought, he didn't think his Mum would be very happy if brought home a new pet without asking her first. How about a fish? That's much easier to take care of and smaller to grow. Yes, he thought, I think I'll start off small and make my own fish. He thought his Mum would let him keep a pet fish, especially one he'd made himself.

So off he went with his friends to Mr Stanton's store cupboard and they helped themselves to a small plastic saucer, which Mr Stanton assured them, was how they had to begin. They were given some odd ingredients for their experiment… one girl was given some yoghurt, a boy was given a bit of potato and Mark was given some liquid (though he was quite pleased about this as he thought the fish would be better off if it was made in liquid). Then, they were told to drop some water on their ingredients and Mr Stanton helped them all put a lid on their saucers, label them with the date and their names so they knew who's dish was whose and finally the dishes were stacked away in the store cupboard.

The rest of the day Mark spent daydreaming about his fish and wondering what colour it would be – could he decide the colour? And what about it's size? Though it must be quite small, given the size of the dish he was to grow in. Oh yes, this was very exciting, learning to grow a pet – he couldn't wait until next month's science lesson when it would be fully grown and ready to take home!

Chapter 2: Litter is Litter

When Mark's Mum came to collect him from school he was very excited and told her all about it. Of course, she thought Mark was either being silly or hadn't listened properly to his teacher but she listened to him anyway and told him that he was quite right, if he created a dog to bring home she would have been a bit cross but if Mark managed to grow a fish, she would be quite happy to buy Mark a fishtank to keep him in. As a treat for showing such an interest in his science lesson, Mark's mum stopped at the corner shop and decided he could choose some sweets as a reward for working hard in school. He chose his favourite, the chewy fruity sweets that come all wrapped separately in a pack – because there were more of them and they would last longer, he thought!

As Mark and his Mum walked home, Mark couldn't resist having a couple of sweets and so he unwrapped one and put it in his mouth, carefully scrunching up the small square bit of paper it had been wrapped in. He looked around for a bin to throw the sweet wrapper in but he couldn't see one at all and his pockets were already full to bursting of all the other important things boys keep in their pockets. Well, it was only a tiny bit of paper after all wasn't it, and if he kept it in his hand he wouldn't be able to unwrap another sweet, which he really wanted to do. So Mark opened his hand to take another sweet and the empty wrapper fell to the ground. And his Mum saw him.

'Mark', she shouted at him, 'don't throw your rubbish away – that's dirty and makes the place look a mess. Put it in the bin not on the floor. If you do that again I won't let you eat any sweets on the way home from school again, whether you've been good or not'.

'But Mum', Mark protested 'I can't see a bin anywhere and my pockets are full. It's only a little wrapper, I'm sure no-one will see it. I only wanted to have another sweet and the wrapper fell out of my hand, I didn't drop it on purpose'.

'Mark, it doesn't matter if you dropped it on purpose or by accident' his Mum explained more gently. 'Litter is litter and eventually all the small pieces become one big mess. If you can't see a bin you should put your rubbish in your pocket. If your pockets are full then you should keep it in your hand until you get home and then put it in the bin'. Then Mark's mum took the rest of the sweets off him to make sure he didn't drop any more rubbish on the ground.

Back at home Mark was a bit upset at having his sweets taken away – he really didn't see how one tiny, little sweet wrapper could be anything to worry about. Especially not in Pinderton, because this was the town where any litter that had been dropped always disappeared by the next morning. He just didn't know how.

Chapter 3: A Fishy Tale

Well the next weeks at school went by quite quickly for Mark as he couldn't stop thinking about his fish, wondering whether it had grown any fins yet, if it had grown it's scales and what colour they were and of course, what it would look like. He thought about different names for it, such as Finlay, Flounder and Gilly but eventually decided not to choose a name just yet until he'd seen it and then he could think of a good name to suit his fish.

After a month, Mr Stanton called everyone around a big table in the middle of the classroom and announced that they would now look at their experiments. One by one he took the dishes out of the cupboard and placed them in the centre of the table where all the children were seated around the edge, full of excitement and wondering what to expect. But when all the dishes had been placed on the table they fell silent; they looked at each other confused – of all the things they were expecting they hadn't expected this.

Mr Stanton shut the store cupboard door and announced cheerily, 'well class, here we are'! Mark peered forward and looked into his dish – there was no fish in there. Quickly he looked along the other dishes in case his label had been stuck to the wrong dish, but there wasn't a fish in any of them. In fact, there were no creatures, no baby animals or anything. Mark felt completely and totally disappointed.

Mr Stanton gave everyone their dish and told them to look closely at what was inside – some people had little bits of furry things, some bluey-green and some white, while Mark could only see tiny little black dots that if you looked closely enough almost looked like they were swimming. Mark decided that not even with the greatest imagination could these black dots be called fish. Oh, he was disappointed – and what would his Mum say when he told her he hadn't grown a fish after all? Now he felt foolish too and cross with Mr Stanton for teasing them – that really wasn't fair and surely teachers weren't allowed to be cruel like that? Looking up at Mr Stanton, Mark decided he didn't like him after all.

Mr Stanton however, still appeared to be excited by this lesson and Mark decided he really had lost the plot when he explained that the furry things in the dish and Marks black dots were the living creatures he'd told them they would create and they could take their dishes home to watch their creations grow! Mark shook his head, sure he had imagined it. A furry little blob of mould in a dish, a living creature? Yes, Mr Stanton had most positively, definitely, lost his marbles.

Chapter 4: Poor Amber (part 1)

The next day was Saturday when a lot of the Pinderton children played outside with their friends. The boys gathered in the fields playing football and enjoying themselves; there was a lot of laughter to be heard, footballs being kicked and shouts of 'goal' echoed through the nearby streets! The girls spent their Saturday's making up dance routines with their friends, singing or playing with their favourite toys. They thought it was boring to kick a ball across a field all day, they preferred to do cartwheels or handstands when they played in the field.

One girl, Amber, was playing with her friends doing just that – dancing and cartwheeling across a field when she suddenly fell over mid-cartwheel and crumpled up in a heap on the grass. 'Urgh', she exclaimed, lifting her hand up and examining it closely.

'Amber, what's the matter, you didn't finish your cartwheel?' one of her friends asked. Then, as she walked closer to help Amber get up, she saw what it was. Slowly, she started walking backwards away from Amber just in case she touched her or fell on her. For do you know what Amber had put her hand in while she was cartwheeling? No? Any idea at all (I'll give you a clue - it was horrid)? No? Then I'll tell you - it was dog poo! Urghh! Squishy, smelly, brown dog poo that had been left right in the middle of the field now covered the palm of her hand and squished through her fingers! Amber started to cry and ran off home with tears running down her face because not only was this the most horrible thing she could have put her hands in but she was embarrassed too – all her friends had seen her with dog poo all over her fingers! She knew the children at school would remember this for a long time and it made her cry even more as she ran home to get cleaned up. Poor Amber.

Chapter 5 : Bright Eyes

Later that evening, as Mark was sitting at home eating his dinner, he heard the rumble of thunder. He loved thunderstorms so quickly ran to the window to see if he could see the dark clouds forming in the sky. But it was very odd – the sky was lovely and clear, there were no thunder clouds anywhere. It was getting a little bit darker now as evening was starting to fall but definitely no thunder clouds. Oh well, he thought, maybe it was a lorry driving by and back to his dinner he went. He was having Shepherds Pie tonight – they were going to have fish and chips but his Mum thought he may not be in the mood for fish after he'd told her all about his science lesson, how Mr Stanton had fooled them all and shown her his experiment dish. She decided it best to avoid the subject of fish for a while until Mark felt better.

The evening passed uneventfully for Mark; he ate his Shepherd's Pie, was allowed to finish his sweets and had a bath ready for bedtime. Just as he was getting his pyjamas on he heard the same rumble of thunder again. 'I'm not imagining this' he thought and ran into his bedroom and tiptoed to his window, which had a lovely view of the park and the field he often played football in. Expecting to see thunder clouds rolling across the sky he looked up but again he couldn't see any big storm clouds, only one small dark cloud just over the swings. He turned round to get into bed, took two steps forwards then stopped, suddenly. A cloud over the swings? That couldn't be right. He went back to the window and saw the dark shape again – it wasn't a cloud, it was far too low and looked solid. Then his eyes opened wide as his mouth fell open and he stood frozen to the spot, leaning on the window sill, peering out into the dusky evening. For in that dark shape, two perfectly round, bright yellow eyes appeared and blinked.

∾

Mark rubbed his eyes and looked again. The yellow eyes were still there but now they were moving slightly, left to right, right to left, almost as if looking for something. Then they rose higher and higher; the higher they rose, the more Mark backed away from the window. Whatever this was, it was alive and he'd seen nothing like it before. He couldn't stop staring at it – it was like a tiny dinosaur but it had funny skin. Some if it looked smooth, some of it looked rough and bumpy and it was different colours. What on earth could it be, he wondered?

Whatever it was, it was definitely looking for something. It stomped slowly towards the bin, peered towards it, raised it's head up as if it was sniffing the air, then quickly turned and lolloped off towards the trees at the edge of the field. Mark was still staring out of the window with his mouth wide-open when his Mum came in to get him to bed.

'Mark, why aren't you in bed yet'? she asked as she entered the room. 'Mum, I just saw something strange in the park' he replied. 'Oh, really, what was that'? 'It was…erm…well, I don't really know what it was actually. I think it was a monster, Mum, but it's disappeared now'. Of course, Mark's Mum thought he was imagining things. 'Well, if it was a monster, at least it wasn't under your bed!' she answered, 'now come on, get into bed and get ready for lights out'.

Mark snuggled down under the duvet cover, his mind whirring, wondering what on earth he could have seen. Was it an alien from a spaceship? Or maybe it was a living dinosaur? Whatever it was he was sure it couldn't have been his imagination, he *saw* those eyes blink, he knew he had.

Chapter 6 : Poor Amber (part 2)

In Amber's house, just down the road and around the corner, she was also getting ready for bed. After she'd run home upset with dog poo all over her hand her Mum had wiped her hand clean and run her a nice, warm bath so she could feel clean all over. To get rid of that horrible lingering pooey smell she's used some of Amber's favourite strawberry scented bubble bath; this always cheered her up; being nice and warm and smelling of strawberries. Amber could almost feel the bubbles washing all the embarrassment of the day down the plughole with them.

As she was getting into her pyjamas she asked her Mum how her accident could happen. 'Why are dogs allowed to poo where we play, Mum? Shouldn't they go and poo somewhere else where we don't play?'

'Well sweetheart, when dogs need a poo they have to go you see, they can't hold it like we can' her Mum explained. 'But, that doesn't mean it should be left lying around. Responsible dog owners carry little plastic bags with them and when their dog has a poo, they pick it up in the little plastic bag and drop it all in the bin. Then there's no poo left behind and no chance of little girls falling into it doing cartwheels!' Amber and her Mum looked at each other then and both chuckled. 'I suppose the owner of the dog that left that poo in the field wasn't very thoughtful or responsible' her Mum continued, 'and sadly Amber, it meant that you suffered because someone else didn't do their duty and clean up after themselves'. Amber decided there and then that if she grew up and had a dog, she would make sure she always had some little doggy bags with her to clear away her dog's messes. And with that in mind, she drifted off to sleep, imagining the type of dog she would like to have, but instead of having a nice dream about clean dogs she ended up dreaming about big smelly poo's that chased her all over town! Poor Amber!

Chapter 7 : At School

The next morning both Mark and Amber were back at school as usual with their friends. Amber didn't have to worry about anybody laughing at her – her friends were very kind and told her how horrible it must have been for her when she fell over and how they wouldn't like it to happen to them. This made her feel much better and quite soon Amber's experience had been forgotten.

Mark was also playing with his best friend Andrew (who was in his class) and they were talking about Mr Stanton's cruel trick he had played, letting them think they were going to grow a pet (Andrew had been hoping to grow a lizard although Mark did think he would have been better to start off with something easier and told him so. They fell out about this for a short while but when neither of them had grown any kind of pet at all they made friends again). 'So what've you done with your science dish Andrew'? Mark asked. 'Oh, I've just put it in my cupboard for now' Andrew replied, 'what have you done with yours?' 'I've left mine on my desk in my room' Mark said, 'I don't know why, I suppose I just don't know what to do with it. My Mum will probably throw it away when she has one of her tidying up days'.

'Anyway Andrew, I've got something much more interesting than that to tell you' Mark began. 'Listen to what I saw last night…'

∽

Mark told Andrew all about the rolls of thunder he heard and the lack of storm clouds. 'Yeah, I heard thunder last night too but it didn't rain' Andrew joined in. 'That's because I don't think it was thunder' Mark continued and told Andrew all about the big yellow eyes, the funny looking skin and the sniffing head. 'Wow, what do you think it was'? Andrew asked, hanging on every word, 'do you think it was giant lizard or something' (Andrew was very interested in dinosaurs and lizards)? 'I just don't know' Mark confessed. 'I've never seen anything like it before but it was weird all right'. Just then the bell rang to end playtime and both Mark and Andrew went back into class, for Andrew's favourite lesson – history.

When history had finished it was dinner-time. Mark and Andrew sat together for their faggots, peas and mashed potatoes, discussing Mark's sighting and making up ideas for what it could be – each idea being even more crazy than the last idea!

'Why don't I ask Mum if we can have a sleep-over soon' suggested Mark 'we can have a midnight feast, watch a film and see if the monster comes back'. Andrew liked the sound of this so when the two boys went home that afternoon they both asked their Mum's if they could have a sleepover and fortunately, they both agreed. It would be next Wednesday so Andrew could go to Mark's house straight from school and have his dinner there and they could walk to school together on Thursday morning. The rest of the school week went quite quickly for Mark and Andrew as they were looking forward to their sleepover, planning what they might do.

Chapter 8 : Fish & Chips

Wednesday came at long last and once school had finally finished, Mark's Dad came to school to pick them up and walk them home. As a treat, Mark's Dad stopped at the corner shop and told them both they could choose a sweet or chocolate bar to eat later on 'as long as you don't spoil your dinner', he added (why do grown-ups keep telling you not to 'spoil your dinner'? Andrew thought, but was far too polite to ask). Andrew chose a small pack of sweets and this time Mark chose a chocolate bar. They played with some toys for a while and Mark showed Andrew his favourite books, toys and his science dish (which despite having several more black dots and blobs of green fur, it still had no fish in it); then Mark's Mum asked them to come downstairs for their dinner. When they got downstairs they couldn't smell anything cooking and when they walked in the kitchen there was nothing in the oven. 'I thought you called us down for dinner'? Mark asked, confused. 'I did', his Mum replied smiling, 'because you've got a friend over tonight I thought you might like some fish and chips'. 'Might like'? Mark thought, *'might* like'? He *loved* fish and chips and he hadn't had any for weeks! Quickly Mark, Andrew and his Mum put their coats on and headed down to the local chip shop. Mark had fish and chips, Andrew had sausage and chips and both Mark's Mum and Dad had roe and chips. As they left the shop with their hot paper bags almost burning their hands they suddenly noticed something they hadn't noticed before. Outside the door of the chip shop, in the street, were lots of bits of paper and little wooden forks – they must have been dropped by people eating their chips, they all thought. But there was also a lot of other rubbish – there were empty cans of pop, plastic bottles of pop, cigarette ends and crisp packets. In fact, they were all very surprised to see such litter – this was Pinderton, and remember, Pinderton doesn't have any litter – or so they thought. So why was there so much rubbish around the doors to the shops and why was the bin outside the chip shop almost empty?

Chapter 9 : Rumbles in the Night

They quickly walked back home so they could eat their chips before they got too cold and after watching one of Andrew's favourite films, Dinotown, the boys got ready for bed. Mark's Mum brought them up some warm milk to help them sleep and after quite a lot of talking and being told to be quiet and get to sleep, both Mark and Andrew drifted off to a happy, peaceful sleep.

Until heavy raindrops and a loud rumble woke them both up with a start. 'What was that'? They both said, jumping up startled. Then the rumble came again, but there was no lightening. 'That's the noise I heard the other night' Mark exclaimed. 'Quick Andrew, come to the window but leave the lights off'. Andrew didn't need telling twice – he was really excited! He quickly jumped out of bed and ran next to Mark who was leaning on the window sill staring out of the window – but he couldn't see anything. All of a sudden, the rumble came again and still no lightening, but this time it sounded much louder and then in the very next second, right in front of their eyes two yellow eyes the size of saucers looked back at them, from the other side of the window.

Mark and Andrew gasped in shock, let go of the window sill and ran to hide behind their beds, the top of their heads just sticking above the duvets, their eyes wide with amazement. The yellow saucer eyes were still there – they blinked twice then moved below the window and out of sight. Mark and Andrew ran back to the window, they couldn't believe it – whatever that was, it had just looked straight at them! Across in the field they found it – rolling on its back just like a dog yet they noticed something very strange. Everytime it rolled, it rolled *over* something, which then vanished once the creature moved. They watched a little longer and yes, they were certain. They saw a few bits of paper blowing across the field in the breeze and a few piles of dog poo, but once this creature walked over them or rolled over them they all disappeared, leaving the field looking clean and tidy. How strange! They looked at each other both as bewildered as the other, then slowly got themselves into bed, so stunned they couldn't even speak.

Chapter 10 : Vanishing Litter

As they walked the short journey to school the next morning they had recovered from the shock of the night before and neither of them could stop talking about the monster. 'What do you reckon it was Andrew'? asked Mark, 'do you think it could have been a baby dinosaur'? 'No, I don't think so' Andrew replied, 'I've never seen a dinosaur quite like that before'. 'Oh, have you seen many dinosaurs then'? Mark asked cheekily, teasing his friend and they both laughed! Andrew meant it was like no *pictures* of dinosaurs he'd ever seen before – of course he'd never seen a *real* dinosaur, he was only eight!

As they walked past the corner shop and the chip shop Andrew suddenly stopped walking and stared at the floor. 'Come on or we'll be late' Mark pointed out. But Andrew didn't move, he just looked at the floor, then up at Mark and then back at the floor again. 'Mark', he began slowly, 'look at this'. Mark looked at the floor with him. 'Look at what'? he asked, 'there's nothing there. Oh hurry up Andrew or we'll be in trouble'.

'I know there's nothing there now' Andrew replied, 'but there was last night, wasn't there? Last night, we saw this area really dirty and messy, with chip paper and cigarettes and all sorts of rubbish lying around'. 'Yes, but now it's tidy again' answered Mark very importantly, 'its always tidy in Pinderton. What's so strange about that?'

'It's strange Mark, because last night this area was very messy and dirty, now it's clean and there's no litter in the litter bins – LOOK!'. Mark took a couple of steps to the bin, peered inside and gasped – Andrew was right, there was absolutely nothing inside the bin. And the bin men hadn't been emptying the bins that morning; bin day was Monday – today was Thursday.

∽

'Don't you think it's strange'? Andrew asked during playtime later that morning, 'That we actually don't see any litter around during the day'? 'Not really,' Mark replied, 'there never is in Pinderton is there? I mean, rubbish does get dropped, it must do, but then it get cleared away doesn't it? By the bin men I suppose. It's not particularly strange, that's just what happens'.

'But it *didn't* happen last night and this morning though, did it'? Andrew continued. 'And that's another thing – they're called *bin* men because they empty the bins – they don't clean the streets *and* the bin men don't come today anyway, so what happened to last night's rubbish outside the shops? And how come the rubbish and poo on the field disappeared when that dinosaur creature rolled over it – do you think he pushed into the ground?'

'I don't know' Mark replied truthfully, 'but one thing I do know and that is that something very strange is going on around here lately. And I'm going to find out what it is'.

Chapter 11 : The Park Visitor

Mark decided that it would be a good idea to start looking at his town with more attention than he usually paid. He had a spare notebook in his drawer that he was going to use to record the changes in his fish, but since that fish was now a disgusting furry green blob which he really must throw away, it was now spare and could be used for other important matters.

He remembered that although he'd only seen this creature twice, on both occasions he had heard a rumble just like thunder a few seconds earlier. He marked down the dates in his book and decided a diary would be the best way to see what happens – he may also be able to use it to work out when the monster might appear next.

Firstly he drew lines down the page so he had four columns to write in. In the first column he wrote the date, in the second column he wrote where he'd seen litter and what it was made up of, in the third column he wrote whether he had either seen the creature or heard the strange rumble and in the last column he wrote whether the rubbish he'd seen earlier was still there. He was sure there must be a link between all these he just wasn't sure what it was, but he soon would, he was determined to.

The next few nights were very quiet and Mark was a little disappointed. He slept all the way through until morning and of course, on his way to school everything was clean and tidy as usual – no litter anywhere.

However, only a few days later all that changed quite considerably – but this time it was in daylight and Mark & Andrew weren't the only people to see it.

2

It was on a Friday and most children were at home because the teachers were having a training day (everybody loved these extra days off school!). As usual, boys were playing football in the field and the girls were dancing and playing in the park when there was another rumble, very loud this time, quickly followed by a roar like a car engine. Suddenly, everybody froze to the spot – even the birds stopped singing. Two seconds later and the rumble came again, this time with very heavy, very clear thudding footsteps.

From behind the trees he appeared, first his nose peeked out, followed by his head then two bright yellow dinner plates of eyes opened and stared down at the children. Very slowly, they all started taking a step back, one at a time until they were almost at the edge of the field where they then turned and fled home, screaming and running as fast as they could. Mark and Andrew also backed away but they didn't run home – instead they backed away to a couple of little low bushes and hid behind these out of sight, watching the creature.

My, how he had grown! Last time his eyes were the size of saucers but now they were the size of dinner plates! His head looked more like a lizard than a dinosaur, Andrew confirmed a little later. His body looked like a stegosaurus and he had a long, thick tail. He had two strong back legs and two thin front arms that didn't quite reach the floor. However, seeing the monster in daylight for the first time, the boys were able to see something absolutely impossible yet true; this creature, this living, breathing, rumbling monster, was made completely and entirely, out of rubbish!

Chapter 12 : What Rubbish!

Almost trying not to breathe lest it should hear them and come after them, Mark and Andrew crouched down behind the bushes and watched. The creature's feet seemed to be made out of paper – newspapers, magazines and chip shop wrappings. As they moved their eyes upwards they examined its arms, which were surprisingly shiny. Squinting to get a better look, these arms appeared to be made out of shiny sweet wrappers and foil, all multicoloured and actually rather pretty in a weird way. Upwards still their eyes travelled, taking in a broad chest made out of cardboard. The chest and body had a brownish look to it but there were green patches too, possibly from mould or from rolling in the grass, it had brown stains over its back and the occasional spots of white and pink which looked remarkably like chewing gum. The head also looked as though it was made of a mixture of cardboard and paper; with it's jaw, nose and top of it's head formed by egg boxes. Out of the lumps and bumps of the egg boxes were those eyes, those huge eyes that shone as brightly as stars at night.

The creature raised its head, sniffed the air and turned to the left, allowing Mark and Andrew the chance to see it's whole body from the side. From the base of it's neck, along the whole of it's body was a row of plastic bottles that stood on end, making it look as though it were a drinks table at a fete! Its body was definitely made of different sorts of paper, small boxes and cardboard, all stuck together with mud and chewing gum. The boys stared in silence, unable to speak even if they dared – for what could you say about this? As their eyes followed the plastic-bottle spine down from its head down to its tail, it transformed into a scary looking strong tail made out of tin cans. As the monster sniffed the air, it swung its tail around, whipping the air as it moved. Mark realised that if you got in the way it would be quite likely that this tail could cause you a serious injury and he made a mental note never to get too close to this incredible creature.

As the monster turned, he unknowingly answered the boy's questions about what happened to litter in Pinderton – it certainly wasn't swept away by a magical cleaning lady who secretly tidied the town during the hours of darkness. The creature thudded his way over to the bins, bent his head down, opened his mouth and out rolled a banana skin tongue that curled around the rubbish that was on the floor, swept it into his mouth where his sharp, foil teeth chewed and then swallowed the rubbish. As soon as he opened his mouth Mark and Andrew nearly choked – the smell that came from the creature was awful. He stank so badly it made them feel quite sick; it was a mixture of rotting food, dirty toilets and sweaty socks.

Once he'd eaten the litter near the bins he marched across the field and found an area where earlier some people had been having a picnic. Of course, there were bottles, papers and wrappings left on the ground – now it was a picnic of another kind! For the second time, Mark and Andrew witnessed the creature drop to his knees, sniff the air then roll around like a dog on the grass, catching everything he rolled in, in his bumpy skin. After what felt like an hour but was actually more likely to have been a minute, Mark and Andrew watched as the creature (which was now slightly fatter having rolled in more litter) firstly got to his knees, then his feet and finally thudded his way back through the trees and out of sight.

Andrew and Mark turned to look at each other then at the exact same time, stood up and ran out of the park as quickly as their legs could carry them.

Chapter 13 : The Litter Critter

'Did you see it, did you see it?' Mark panted, as soon as they'd run back into the safety of his house, bolting the door behind them. Both of them, nearly breathless from running so quickly, could hardly speak and they were gasping for breath.

'Of course I saw it', Andrew replied ' I couldn't miss it! It was right there – right in front of us. It's real – and I know what it is Mark, I know what it is!'

Mark's eyes opened wide, he was desperate to know. Andrew knows all about dinosaurs and lizards and such creatures so he knew his friend would know more than he would. 'Well' he prompted him eagerly, 'what is it? Is it a dinosaur or something come to life? Tell me, tell me'! Mark was almost hopping up and down with excitement.

Andrew said nothing but walked over the chest of drawers where Mark's failed fish experiment lay sadly on the top, all green and furry and now almost filling the dish completely. He remained silent and lifted the dish, peered at it closely, inspecting it as he moved it around looking through the sides, through the bottom of the dish and through the lid before finally placing it back on the drawers. He slowly turned to Mark and quietly declared 'it's a Litter Critter'.

'A what'? Mark responded. 'A Litter Critter' Andrew repeated confidently, 'a living creature that's made entirely out of litter. We saw it – there wasn't one bit of it that was made of anything else. Plus, we saw him eat the litter by the bins. I'll bet that's what he's doing when he rolls on the floor – as he rolls on the rubbish, it sticks to the chewing gum and the other rubbish and that's how he grows. I've read about them in fairytales when I was smaller but I didn't think they existed until now. I can't believe it's real but it's definitely a Litter Critter'.

'Hang on', Mark queried, 'if it's a litter critter and he eats rubbish, why didn't he just eat the rubbish from the bin? Why only eat the rubbish on the floor? That doesn't make sense'.

'Think about it', Andrew insisted. 'Look at how big he was – his jaw was too big to get inside the bin. Perhaps he did eat out of the bins when he was smaller but as he's grown he's become too big for his own good and that's why we've been hearing him. Those rumbles must have been his stomach rumbling because he was hungry – not rumbles of thunder. If he's been rolling around in litter he's been growing and growing and now he's too big to eat out of the bins, he's eating off the ground'.

'But how did he come to be, though'? Mark asked. What Andrew was saying actually made sense but it was all so strange and abnormal, he was having difficulty understanding it all. Andrew picked up the science dish and held it out at arms length for Mark to see. 'Here's your answer', he said mysteriously.

2

'We thought Mr Stanton was having us on about creating life, but he wasn't' Andrew explained. 'When he told us we would create life we thought he meant some kind of creature, but he never actually told us exactly *what* we would be creating, did he? Look Mark, look at the dish'. Slowly, Mark took two steps forward and lifted the dish out of Andrew's hand. It certainly looked different now – it was much bigger, greener and a lot furrier. 'I think it's mould, but it's *grown*, that's the point. Anything that grows has to be living, doesn't it? We did create life Mark, just not in the way we expected!'

Mark let this bit of information sink in first and although he realised that Andrew was right and Mr Stanton hadn't lost his marbles after all, it still didn't answer how Pinderton had managed to grow a living, breathing enormous litter critter. As he pointed this out to Andrew, the answer dawned on them both. What did the Litter Critter and their science experiment have in common? They both began as left over rubbish of course!

Chapter 14 : The Birth of a Litter Critter

Of course, that was the answer! The Litter Critter was made out of rubbish that people had thrown away and not put in the bin – during the night he came out and ate or rolled in the rubbish, growing bigger and stronger himself and of course, keeping the town clean at the same time! Mr Stanton had given them all small pieces of litter to put in their dishes for the 'life experiment' (as he had called it back then). Now, litter on it's own doesn't just come to life obviously, and neither Mark nor Andrew believed in magic (not now that they realised the town wasn't cleaned by a magical cleaning lady) so there must be something that happened to both the science dishes and the Litter Critter, but what was it? After five minutes of hard thinking, Mark suddenly jumped up with a grin on his face. 'I've got it' he announced proudly, 'it's water'!

'Water'? Andrew asked, then 'of course – everything needs water to live!' 'Yes,' agreed Mark, 'and that's exactly what they've both had. Remember, just before we sealed the lids, we all dropped a couple of drops of water in our dish? That must have been it – the water must have started it growing…' '…and if the Litter Critter lives outdoors', continued Andrew, 'then he gets his water from…'

'RAIN'! they both shouted together! That was it – the mystery solved! Rain falling on people's discarded rubbish left on the ground had begun to grow mould until eventually, there was so much fur and tiny dots of life that they all joined together and the rubbish began to slowly move on it's own. As it came across other pieces of litter, they stuck to the mould, slowly growing and getting bigger each day. With every rainfall, each bit of rubbish began to multiply until the creature was formed – this was why Mark thought it looked bigger the second time he saw it – because it *had* grown bigger! Now the problem was what to do about it and so far only Mark and Andrew completely knew of its existence. The other children that had seen it in the park that day didn't yet know what it was or anything about it and Mark was sure that nobody would have believed them if they told anyone. After all, grown-ups hardly ever listen to children, do they?

Chapter 15 : The School Visitor

Now that they knew about the Litter Critter and how it was able to grow, both Mark and Andrew were very careful not to drop any litter. Even when their pockets were full to bursting, they would squeeze in any rubbish in their pockets as much as they could. They were scared of the Litter Critter – it didn't look or sound very friendly and it smelt awful. They'd both told their parents what they'd seen and explained the whole story, including how they thought it had grown from rubbish and rain – they even told a couple of their very best friends, but sadly, nobody believed them. Their parents told them it was a good story but they were getting too old to believe in monsters and their friends accused them of telling stories and being silly. After this, they decided it was best to keep their secret to themselves – but at least they could share it with each other. They were thankful it only seemed to appear at the park where they were very close to their safe, warm homes, should they need to run away from it in a hurry.

Until one day…

It was a dull, rainy Thursday when the bell went for morning playtime. A Hall Monitor came into the classroom upstairs where Mark and Andrew's class was located, and announced that because it was now raining outside, it was a wet playtime. The whole class groaned – everyone hated wet playtime because it meant playing games or talking in the classroom when they would have much rather been running around in the playground. The teachers didn't like it much either, because they had to spend their break in the classroom with their noisy class, rather than drinking coffee with the other teachers in the Staff-Room.

Outside it was misty, cold and dark and the rain lashed against the windows and rolled down the glass endlessly. No-one thought much of it when, along with the noise of the raindrops a little rumble growled over the school. It was just the sort of weather for a storm. On and on it rained until the bell rang again to signal the end of playtime and the start of more lessons.

Mark and Andrew were having an Art lesson this morning, their tables were covered with newspaper, glue, pipe-cleaners, card, scissors and brightly-coloured paper. It was a huge mess but everyone was enjoying themselves – they all liked lessons where they could do things much more than the lessons where they had to sit still and listen (like history, Mark thought, although he didn't say that to Andrew as he knew history was his friends favourite subject). Again, another rumble rolled overhead and a couple of children seated near the window looked out, waiting for a flash of lightening. Instead, a loud gasp came from across the classroom and chairs scraped back across the floor. As Mark and Andrew looked up from their table to see what was happening, they saw three of their class-mates backing away from the window towards the door. Mark and Andrew looked at each other for a moment, each realising what the noise was. They ran to the window for confirmation and there, to answer their expectations, were two huge, shiny yellow eyes staring in through the window straight at them.

Chapter 16 : The Headteacher's Office

'That's him, that's the Litter Critter' Mark shouted excitedly at his class, 'that's what Andrew and I told you about. He's made of rubbish but I've never seen him anywhere but the park or fields before!'

The teacher stood up, wondering what all the commotion was about, and strode over to the window. As he looked out, he too saw the two huge yellow eyes that slowly tilted to one side, as if examining him, then righted themselves and blinked.

'Class, everyone, step away from the windows, slowly' he ordered, wondering what on earth this strange creature was that was in the playground, that could clearly, easily peer through an upstairs window.

He gathered the class in the corridor and sent someone to fetch the Headteacher. When the Headteacher arrived, Mark strained to hear them talking, wondering what they were saying. Although he couldn't clearly hear them, he did manage to hear that the Headteacher had also seen the Litter Critter; he then heard his name and both the Headteacher and his teacher looked at him, before calling out his name and asking him to step forwards.

Nervously, Mark stepped forwards in front of the class and stood before his teacher and the Headteacher. 'Follow me please Mark', was all that the Headteacher said, before turning and walking back towards his office. 'Stay here, the rest of you', Mark heard his teacher telling the rest of the class behind him. Now he was in trouble, he thought. He wasn't sure why, but there was only one reason you were ever asked by the Headteacher to go to his office and it was never a good sign.

∽

'Now Mark', he began ('here it comes', thought Mark), your teacher has just told me something rather strange and interesting. Apparently, when your classmates saw what was in the playground and backed away, I hear that you and your friend Andrew ran to the window and declared that you know what this creature is. Is that correct'?

'Yes, sir' he replied, wondering if the Headteacher thought he had brought the creature to school himself and that he was in trouble for that.

'Then, would you please enlighten me with what we have in our school playground and what we should do about it'? Mark looked up, confused for a moment. 'Sir - pardon?' he whispered, almost afraid to speak.

'I'm asking you if you know what this creature is and if you do, do you know what it wants'? he repeated. Mark realised he wasn't in trouble after all – in fact, the Headteacher of his school was asking him for information, for help! He should be very proud, not scared!

'Well, I'm not sure why it's here exactly' Mark began, 'but I can tell you what it is. Andrew and I discovered it recently and it's a Litter Critter'. Mark and his Headteacher sat down in his office and Mark told him the whole story, from seeing him in the park the first night, then how he'd grown and what he looked like and finally how he and Andrew believe he came to life.

'That's quite a story there young Mark' began the Headteacher 'and if I hadn't just seen it with my own eyes I wouldn't have believed it. But it's real and we need to do something about it now. It must have come to your window because you were doing art – if the rumble was it's stomach rumbling because he's hungry, your classroom must have looked like a buffet to him!' Mark couldn't help smiling as he pictured the Litter Critter sitting down at his table, having a buffet with his arts and craft materials! He realised at that point, he had a very special and understanding Headteacher. 'I believe' continued the Head, 'this calls for an emergency assembly'.

Chapter 17 : Emergency Assembly

Word spread quickly and soon all the school had gathered in the Hall for an emergency assembly. Seated in their classes, the teachers stood at the front of the hall with Mark and the Headteacher standing in he doorway. The Headteacher walked out in front of everyone, stood in the middle of the teachers, and declared an emergency situation. 'We have an unwelcome visitor, boys and girls' he began. 'There is no need to be alarmed but I have somebody here who can tell you much more than I can about him. I ask you all to listen and pay attention to what you are about to hear. Mark, would you come to the front please?'

Mark's head spun and he felt instantly giddy – stand at the front of an assembly? On his own? Suddenly he felt very small and nervous, his throat incredibly dry. 'Sir', he asked quietly, 'would it be alright if Andrew comes too please'? Understanding this was rather frightening for a child, the Headteacher agreed – after all, Andrew knew just as much as Mark did and perhaps the rest of the children would listen more if two boys told their tale. 'Of course', he replied, 'Andrew, would you please step to the front too?'

Between them, as they began to tell the others about the Litter Critter and how it lives off rubbish, Mark and Andrew became less nervous and more confident as they realised everyone in the whole school was sitting silently, watching them and listening to their every word.

∽

When they had finished informing the school about the Litter Critter, the Headteacher made everybody very happy when he declared that he thought it would be better if they all went home, for the school couldn't be considered safe with a huge monster in the playground, could it? He and the other teachers contacted all the parents and guardians, who soon arrived at the school gates ready to take them home. Typically, by the time the parents had reached the school, the Litter Critter had long gone. They thought at first it was a joke and it took some time for the Headteacher and other teachers to explain it was no joke and they were worried about the safety of the children. Gradually, one by one, the parents accepted that although this was a very odd situation they did need to take the children home, though they couldn't imagine what on earth the fuss was all about. Until ten minutes later, when they found out for themselves.

Chapter 18 : Daylight Outing

It was still raining by this time so as people started to walk home from the school, a lot of people put their umbrellas up to keep dry. As Mark and his Dad turned the corner at the bottom of School Road, the noise came again. The rumble.

'We'll have to hurry Mark', his Dad said, 'otherwise we'll get caught in a thunderstorm too and we don't want to be out in thunder and lightening with an umbrella up, it's dangerous'. 'Dad, I really don't think that's thunder' Mark protested, 'That's the Litter Critter. It's hungry again and it's after food'.

'Look, I know what your teachers said earlier Mark, but I think they were pulling your leg. I'm sure there's another reason we have to take you home and perhaps we'll find out later what it was. For now, let's just get home before the storm starts and get ourselves dry'. So on they walked, Mark trying to persuade his Dad that the Litter Critter was real, his Dad more concerned that they hurry home before they got too wet.

As they walked up the road they noticed a bad smell, Mark's Dad commented that the rainwater must have filled up the drains and that's where the smell was coming from. However, Amber and her mum were walking a little way behing Mark and they both recognised the smell instantly – it was the same smell that Amber had to wash away in the bath – it was the strong, sickly unmistakable smell of fresh dog poo. As they all turned the final corner to take them past the park, Mark, his Dad, Amber and her Mum stopped walking and almost froze to the spot. There, right in front of him, was the Litter Critter, standing in the field.

'See Dad, I told you' stated Mark proudly, 'but we have to get home quickly before he sees us. If he turns stay away from his tail, it's made of tin cans and could really hurt if it catches you'. But there were several more people standing behind Mark and his Dad, all of them looking at this huge, impossible creature in front of them. They'd been told by their children that Mark and Andrew knew the most about the monster and now they had heard Mark telling his Dad about it's tail. He obviously knew a lot more than anyone else and now they were scared too – they wanted to know more. Amber was worried in case it was the monster's poo that she had fallen in, now she'd seen it and smelt it again!

'I know that smell' cried Ambers Mum, 'that monster's covered in dog poo! Don't go near it'! Amber clung to her Mum and started to get upset, she was very scared.

'We need a town meeting', a voice shouted from somewhere in the distance. 'Let's all go to the Town Hall', agreed another. 'That boy knows what this is and we need to know too' another voice from the back joined in. 'TOWN HALL EVERYBODY, NOW!'

So everybody ran in the opposite direction to the park where the Litter Critter was now tromping through the field, to the safety and warm space of Pinderton Town Hall.

Once inside, they bolted the doors shut and the elderly ladies put on the kettle and made everybody cups of tea and orange squash for the children. Mark felt a nudge on his arm – he looked and his Dad was nudging him with his elbow. 'If you know what this is, you need to tell everybody', his Dad advised him. 'I'll come with you but I think we should stand on the stage and inform the town what this is and what it wants, before people become too scared to do anything'. Realising his Dad was right, Mark walked to the stage at the front of the Town Hall and coughed. Nobody took any notice, they were all too busy talking and panicking; all Mark could hear was a loud, wordless babble of noise.

BANG BANG, BANG! The babble quickly stopped and everyone fell silent then turned to the stage, where Mark's Dad was holding the broom he had banged on the floor to get their attention.

'Listen everyone' his Dad began, 'my son knows what this creature is, where it came from and what it wants. He'll tell you all now so please be quiet and listen to what he has to say'. Wow, Mark thought, he believes me! Mark took a step forward, cleared his throat with a little cough and stepped into the limelight.

Chapter 19 : Town Hall Meeting

For the third time that day, Mark again recalled the story of the Litter Critter; his first sighting from his bedroom window looking out at the park, his second close-up sighting with Andrew in the park, the close encounter from the classroom window to today's appearance which they had all seen and smelt.

Although everybody found it incredibly hard to believe, they too had seen it and therefore what Mark was saying must be true. They'd heard and seen this creature too! But why was it here and what could they do about it?

As soon as he had finished speaking, Mark was bombarded with questions. 'What is it eating then?'; 'Will it go away?'; 'Is it dangerous – will it try to eat us?'; 'Are there any more of them?' and so on. It all became a little too much for Mark, all these questions being asked at once until 'BANG BANG BANG!' In came Mark's Dad with his broom again to quieten everybody down.

'Mark has told you everything he knows so far', interrupted his Dad. 'If you have any questions, please ask one at a time and he will try to answer. If he can't answer them do not be angry – he is just the same as you and I except that he'd seen this creature before. That's the only difference so please be understanding. He may not have all your answers'.

The questions became more orderly then and Mark found he was able to answer most of them fairly easily. Until one was asked: 'But why is it here now and what does it want? If it usually comes out at night, why is it now coming out in the daytime and why is it now coming into the town?' This stumped Mark, he really didn't know the answer to that one. So he was very surprised and grateful when a familiar voice from the crowd answered 'I can answer that'.

Chapter 20 : The Solution

Andrew stepped forwards and smiled at his friend. 'Of course' Mark thought, 'I bet Andrew's figured something else out and hasn't had chance to tell me with all the fuss of today'. Andrew stood at the front of the hall next to his friend and began to explain what he thought was the reason for it coming out in the daytime.

'As you know, this creature is made of rubbish, which is why it's called a Litter Critter. It is important to know that without litter it would not be able to live. So it is here because of us – we have created it by dropping litter.

When it was small, we wouldn't have noticed it at all. We may have seen him and thought it was a mouse or a rat. But as he rolls in litter, chewing gum sticks to him and more litter then sticks to the gum, which is how he grows. He stinks because when he rolls in the ground everything he rolls in sticks to him, so he *is* covered in dog poo. Obviously the bigger he gets, the hungrier he gets too, which is why we've been hearing his tummy rumble lately. He can eat both paper rubbish and left over food, like apple cores, stale sandwiches, banana skins, cold chips and crisps but these are rotten, that's why the smell becomes even worse when he opens his mouth. He's getting bigger and needing more food so he's now coming out in the daytime aswell to look for food. That's what he was doing at school – looking for paper and food leftovers to eat. Remember, he came to our window when we were having an art lesson – to him it was all food. There's no danger whatsoever that he may try to eat us, he lives entirely off rubbish. The only danger to us is if he steps on us or knocks us over with his tail – he can easily hurt us but won't try to eat us. The main point to realise is that while there is rubbish lying around, there will be a Litter Critter around.'

'So what do we do' asked a man from the town 'How can we stop him?'

'The only way to stop him' Mark replied, 'is to make sure we don't drop any litter. If there is no litter on the floor he will not be able to grow. If he stops growing he will stop being so hungry and then stop looking for food or more rubbish'.

'But surely he'll just eat of the bins, won't he?' a young woman queried.

'Actually, no.' Andrew answered. 'His head and jaw are too big to fit into the bins which is why he is living off food dropped on the ground. As long as litter is put into the bins he will have nothing to eat and will start to waste away to nothing, before eventually disappearing altogether'.

'But how can that happen' a small child asked 'How can he disappear forever?'

Mark smiled as he realised he knew the answer. 'When paper dries, it can fall off whatever it was stuck to', he began. 'As long as the Litter Critter stops growing there is no new rubbish to keep him strong. The old rubbish will soon start to loosen and fall off, especially when it's windy. The Litter Critter will then start to shrink as his body falls apart'.

'What we *must* do', continued Andrew, 'is to make sure that any litter that falls off the litter critter is put straight into a bin. That's the only way to make sure he doesn't come back and to stop another Critter from being born'.

'Then we need to have a 'Litter Patrol' suggested the Mayor. 'Let's all make sure everyday, we have a rota and for one hour a day, the patrol make sure every bit of litter they find is put in a bin.' 'We agree' a policeman added 'and we'll make a Law to tell everybody that they must make sure they put their litter in a bin. If they don't, they have to pay a fine, which will go to help the Litter Patrols.'

Now the town understood what the Litter Critter was and realising it was of their own making, having agreed a solution they left the Town Hall feeling much happier than when they had run in earlier, screaming. They had a plan and knew that as long as they stuck to it, they could defeat the Litter Critter and make sure no more Critters were born.

∽

So next time you have a little piece of rubbish, remember this story. It only takes one spot of litter to grow a Critter. The Litter Patrols are still there working hard but now they patrol every town, not just Pinderton; have a look for them one day you can see them wearing bright yellow vests picking up litter with a grabbing stick. After all, no town wants a dirty, smelly, scary Litter Critter do they? And just in case you thought this story was made up - ask a policeman what he would do if he saw someone drop any litter…

The End

Lightning Source UK Ltd.
Milton Keynes UK
177591UK00001B/307/P